Acting Edition

I0584521

Meteor Shower

by Steve Martin

ISBN 978-0-573-70702-5

www.concordtheatricals.com
www.concordtheatricals.co.uk

FOR PRODUCTION INQUIRIES

UNITED STATES AND CANADA
info@concordtheatricals.com
1-866-979-0447

UNITED KINGDOM AND EUROPE
licensing@concordtheatricals.co.uk
020-7054-7298

Each title is subject to availability from Concord Theatricals Corp.,
depending upon country of performance. Please be aware that
METEOR SHOWER may not be licensed by Concord Theatricals Corp.
in your territory. Professional and amateur producers should contact
the nearest Concord Theatricals Corp. office or licensing partner to
verify availability.

No one shall make any changes in this title(s) for the purpose of production. No part of this book may be reproduced, stored in a retrieval system, scanned, uploaded, or transmitted in any form, by any means, now known or yet to be invented, including mechanical, electronic, digital, photocopying, recording, videotaping, or otherwise, without the prior written permission of the publisher. No one shall share this title(s), or any part of this title(s), through any social media or file hosting websites.

For all inquiries regarding motion picture, television, online/digital and other media rights, please contact Concord Theatricals Corp.

MUSIC AND THIRD-PARTY MATERIALS USE NOTE

Licensees are solely responsible for obtaining formal written permission from copyright owners to use copyrighted music and/or other copyrighted third-party materials (e.g. artworks, logos) in the performance of this play and are strongly cautioned to do so. If no such permission is obtained by the licensee, then the licensee must use only original music and materials that the licensee owns and controls. Licensees are solely responsible and liable for clearances of all third-party copyrighted materials, including without limitation music, and shall indemnify the copyright owners of the play(s) and their licensing agent, Concord Theatricals Corp., against any costs, expenses, losses and liabilities arising from the use of such copyrighted third-party materials by licensees. For music, please contact the appropriate music licensing authority in your territory for the rights to any incidental music.

IMPORTANT BILLING AND CREDIT REQUIREMENTS

If you have obtained performance rights to this title, please refer to your licensing agreement for important billing and credit requirements.

The Original Broadway Production of *METEOR SHOWER* was produced by Joey Parnes, Sue Wagner, John Johnson, James L. Nederlander, The John Gore Organization, Scott Rudin, Eli Bush, FG Productions, Jamie deRoy, Sally Horchow, Sharon Karmazin, Barbara Manocherian, JABS Theatricals, Ergo Entertainment, Seth A. Goldstein, Elm City Productions, Diana DiMenna, Jay Alix & Una Jackman, Jennifer Manocherian, Cricket Jiranek, Catherine Adler & Marc David Levine, and The Shubert Organization.

The World Premiere Production of *METEOR SHOWER* was produced by The Old Globe (Barry Edelstein, Artistic Director; Michael G. Murphy, Managing Director) and Long Wharf Theatre (Gordon Edelstein, Artistic Director; Joshua Borenstein, Managing Director).

METEOR SHOWER premiered on Broadway on November 29, 2017 at the Booth Theatre in New York City. The performance was directed by Jerry Zaks, with scenic design by Beowulf Boritt, costume design by Ann Roth, lighting design by Natasha Katz, and sound design by Fitz Patton. The production stage manager was J. Jason Daunter. The cast was as follows:

CORKY . . . . Amy Schumer

NORM . . . . Jeremy Shamos

GERALD . . . . Keegan-Michael Key

LAURA . . . . Laura Benanti

CHARACTERS

CORKY
NORM
GERALD
LAURA

AUTHOR'S NOTES

This play has been performed both on a proscenium stage and in the round. In the round, the revelation of the meteor strike on the chaise lounge is simultaneous with the strike. In proscenium, the hole in the lounge is revealed in a subsequent scene.

In the "the bug flux has been achieved" scene there are two timings that can be used for the water that comes out of Norm's stomach. One is to do it as written. The other is to save the water effect for the very end of the scene when everything is truly chaotic. Both versions have been performed successfully.

"Chamois" is pronounced "shammy." I mention this because the issue has come up more than once.

The play is performed without an intermission.

Scene One

*(A modern house in Ojai, California,
early evening, August 1993.* **CORKY** *enters
polishing coffee spoons, which she sets on
a side table. Her husband,* **NORM**, *hurried,
enters from the bedroom, still in the process of
getting dressed.)*

*(If projection is possible, right before curtain,
three separate cards should announce:)*

[Ojai, California.]

[August 1993.]

[83°.]

CORKY. Norm, they're here in fifteen minutes.

NORM. I'm going crazy. Help me.

CORKY. What?

> *(**NORM** is exasperated. He's trying to remember
> something.)*

NORM. I'm trying to think...this book title. It's for *Jeopardy*...

> *(Indicates the TV back in the bedroom.)*

It's...oh...the tip of my tongue. Something like...Death
to the Cuckoo. But not that...com'n...book title. It's like
Death to the Cuckoo...

CORKY. *To Kill a Mockingbird.*

NORM. Thank you! Thank you! How'd you come up with
that?

CORKY. I know your brain.

NORM. And yet another reason to be married.

CORKY. You'd repressed it, that's all.

NORM. Yeah. And when I repress something, I push it way down and kick dirt over it. It's not coming back.

(He puts on his pants.)

CORKY. If you don't deal with your subconscious, it will deal with you.

NORM. That's good. Who said that?

CORKY. In that book, remember?

NORM. Oh yeah.

CORKY. You want a pre-wine?

NORM. A what?

CORKY. A pre-wine. A wine before the wine. Doesn't count.

NORM. Doesn't count?

CORKY. Not if it's before the guests come. Doesn't count.

NORM. Then what's the problem?

*(**NORM** takes a sip of wine.)*

(Sees the eggplants.) What are these?

CORKY. Eggplants. Arrived this afternoon. No note.

NORM. Must be from the Newmans.

CORKY. Thoughtful.

NORM. I guess.

CORKY. What's *she* like?

NORM. I don't know her; just him. She was a West Coast editor at *Vogue* for three years. She seemed fine.

CORKY. You met her?

NORM. She was picking up Gerald after tennis. She's the one who mentioned the meteor shower.

CORKY. Oh.

(Then.) How does a meteor shower come up in conversation?

NORM. She said Gerald wanted to leave town to see this meteor shower, first I had heard of it. So he puffs up – kept calling it a rain of fire, can't miss the rain of fire, once in a lifetime, blah blah, and I said we live in Ojai and he said can you see stars there and I said, "Yeah, shopping on the weekends."

(CORKY stares.)

And he looked at me like that...

(Points to her face.)

...but she laughed.

CORKY. You liked that.

NORM. Well, yeah. She got the joke.

CORKY. I read people know if they want to sleep with a person within two seconds of meeting them. I believe it. Do you?

NORM. I could see that.

CORKY. *(Miffed.)* Oh yeah well that's fine.

NORM. I didn't mean I wanted to... You said you believed it.

CORKY. I said I read it; you said you believed it.

NORM. No, I didn't say I believed it; I said I could see it.

CORKY. Oh, so you can see the moon but you don't believe the moon.

NORM. What?

CORKY. *(Relaxing.)* Hey, remember the summer I believed in crystals?

NORM. *(Laughs a bit.)* Yeah. And how about me? In college I had a moment with the power of pyramids.

CORKY. Put a weapon in the hand of a stupid belief and it kills you.

NORM. Wow. That's a thought. Who said that?

CORKY. I did.

NORM. You did?

CORKY. Why?

NORM. It's clever. It just doesn't sound like you.

(CORKY, hurt, steps toward him and enters a "talking mode." NORM goes to meet her. They hold hands and face each other. They've done this a hundred times.)

CORKY. I love you and I know you love me.

NORM. *(Quoting CORKY back to her.)* You said, "I love you and I know you love me."

CORKY. I understand you probably did not know you hurt me.

NORM. You said, "I probably did not know I hurt you." That's what you meant?

CORKY. Yes. I'm asking you to be more careful with my feelings. They are not playthings.

NORM. Your feelings are not playthings. That's what you meant?

CORKY. Yes.

NORM. I'm sorry that I hurt you in this way. I hope that you understand that I did not intend to hurt you, and I will try to use that particular joking manner less often.

CORKY. I do understand.

(*Then.*) How come she's not with *Vogue* anymore?

NORM. No clue. I met her for five seconds.

CORKY. I hope they like our place.

NORM. Are you kidding, this place could be in *Architectural Digest*. I love the furniture, I love the pillows, I love everything about it.

CORKY. *He* sounds nice.

NORM. He is nice.

CORKY. I don't like *her*.

NORM. What? Why?

CORKY. I don't know. The *Vogue* thing. What was she wearing?

NORM. I can't remember. A top...a black top, pencil skirt... is that what they call it?

CORKY. It is if that's what it was.

NORM. Brunette. Stylish. Big hair. *[This description can change to suit the actress.]*

CORKY. Sexy?

NORM. Not in the least.

CORKY. So she was.

NORM. A bit.

CORKY. Thank you for being considerate.

NORM. I honor your feelings.

CORKY. And him?

NORM. Him. He's hard to describe, kind of two people. Can be vicious on the tennis court if he's behind, then if he's ahead, wonderful guy. Likes to pontificate. I figure for one night it could be interesting, and he seems very connected. Could be good for us.

CORKY. Your instincts are always good.

NORM. I really appreciate your attitude on this.

CORKY. I acknowledge your appreciation.

NORM. *(Picks up his glass.)* A bit more wine.

CORKY. Maybe you should wait.

NORM. Good idea. Don't want to peak too early.

CORKY. Or not at all.

> *(He looks at her.)*

I'm so sorry…

NORM. I honor that you're sorry.

CORKY. I honor and cherish you as a person.

NORM. I need to be in my cave now.

CORKY. Yes.

> *(She exits to the kitchen. He picks up a newspaper from a low table. Looks at a circled column.)*

NORM. *(Reads aloud, to himself.)* …From the northern sky. Tonight, fifty to sixty meteors are expected per hour. It has been suggested that life on this planet could have been generated by meteors striking the earth…

> *(Lights fade.)*

Scene Two

(CORKY, NORM, GERALD, and LAURA are in the living room, mid-conversation. GERALD is standing.)

GERALD. A billion-year-old light show. Piercing the atmosphere, bursting with radiance.

LAURA. Nice.

GERALD. Caught in our gravitational pull, some grazing the atmosphere, some in a death spiral heading for Earth.

LAURA. Go, baby.

GERALD. Everyone thinks of meteors as something that happen at night. But they're striking the earth during the day too, but of course we can't see them can we... *(Then.)* Can we?

(More urgent.) Can we?

CORKY. Oh, you want... I see, well I think...

GERALD. *(Points to NORM.)* I want him to answer.

NORM. Oh. Uh, no no we can't. Because of the sun...

GERALD. *(Walks to CORKY, gently touches her.)* Because of the sun, exactly. The brightness of the sun overwhelms the dimness of the meteor. Like the way some personalities overwhelm the lesser lights.

CORKY. I never thought of it that way.

GERALD. How about you, Norm?

NORM. What?

GERALD. Ever think of it that way?

NORM. I don't really know that I di...

GERALD. I thought of it that way when I was sixteen.

NORM. Huh.

GERALD. See, meteors represent the conjunction of two very different worlds. Like the bug flux.

CORKY. The bug flux?

GERALD. Yes, right here in California, too. You have the mountain bugs that love the mountains, and the coastal bugs that love the coast. But where they meet and mingle is called the bug flux, and it's chaos. In a way, we're the coastal bugs who came to visit you, the mountain bugs.

NORM. Hors d'oeuvres?

> *(He picks them up and offers the plate to everyone.* **GERALD** *takes one.)*

GERALD. Love to.

> *(He offers the plate to* **LAURA***, who responds.)*

LAURA. *(Referencing her figure.)* Noooo.

GERALD. Hmm. Tasty. What is this?

CORKY. Petrale crab. From Chile.

GERALD. Delicious.

LAURA. We loved this invitation.

GERALD. Can't tell you. We can't see the sky in Santa Barbara. Just the little light from the city blocks out everything.

LAURA. And Corky. Norm has told me so much about you.

CORKY. He has? He said he hadn't talked to you that mu...

LAURA. Oh, did I misspeak?

> **(CORKY** *checks* **NORM***; he looks befuddled. Then:)*

CORKY. How did you like being an editor at *Vogue*?

LAURA. Oh...oh...it was fabulous. Then the LA office closed.

CORKY. Oh! Where in LA? We used to live there.

LAURA. Uptown.

CORKY. Uptown? There is no uptown in LA.

LAURA. *(Looking around at the house.)* Gerald, look at this place...so charming. This is exactly what we need. A little nothing out in the country.

> *(Awkward moment.)*

CORKY. That dress is so nice.

LAURA. Oh, thank you. I just get tired of looking awful. Don't you?

NORM. *(After a beat, to* **GERALD.***)* How long have you been interested in the heavens?

GERALD. Who said I was interested in the heavens? I'm interested in the *metaphor* of the heavens. Example: I flew in a plane once to follow a solar eclipse.

CORKY. That must have been beautiful.

GERALD. Beautiful? Powerful. To block out the sun? To be a man and block out the sun longer than nature intended? I defeated the sun. I thought, "I'm something to contend with." Should I go on?

CORKY. Oh, yes!

GERALD. Well, now I feel on the spot.

> *(He sits, stands immediately.)*

Anyway...

> *(Lights out.)*

Scene Three

*(Same scene as Scene One, a jump backward in time. **NORM** in same position as when he was reading the paper. Their guests haven't arrived yet.)*

NORM. ...From the northern sky. Tonight, fifty to sixty meteors are expected per hour. It has been suggested that life on this planet could have been generated by meteors striking the earth...

CORKY. *(Entering with a snack tray.)* Tell me more about... is it Gerald?

NORM. Yeah. Delightful. Life of the party. Anyway...they know the Coopers.

CORKY. They know the Coopers?

NORM. Yeah. And we should meet the Coopers. It's just good business to meet the Coopers.

CORKY. *(Gossipy.)* Did you hear about the Coopers?

NORM. What?

CORKY. About him.

NORM. What?

CORKY. Went berserk.

NORM. Really? Where'd you hear this?

CORKY. I was told he just cracked up about four months ago. Strange. They said it had something to do with produce.

NORM. Produce?

CORKY. Yeah, like corn or lettuce. I heard there was a woman involved too.

NORM. Well, he's getting older, midlife crisis. He probably felt ignored.

CORKY. Oh, poor guy. Try being a woman. One day, you notice men aren't looking anymore.

NORM. I don't believe that. I see men looking at you.

CORKY. That's sweet.

NORM. Eyes.

> (**NORM** *indicates she didn't look into his eyes*
> *when she spoke. She resets and looks into his*
> *eyes.*)

CORKY. That's sweet.

(Then.) You ever been interested in a somebody else?

NORM. I don't care about that.

CORKY. You can't not.

NORM. I don't think about it.

CORKY. I read that men are programmed.

NORM. I read that article. It was in "Let's Ruin a Perfectly Happy Marriage" magazine. I'm also programmed not to humiliate you.

CORKY. I love that. You just allayed my anxiety.

NORM. No woman is coming. The only thing coming for us is the Newmans.

> *(Lights out.)*

Scene Four

(Back to Scene Two, **GERALD** *and* **LAURA** *have entered the room.* **CORKY** *holds a tray of drinks.* **NORM** *offers his hand.)*

NORM. Welcome.

CORKY. You found us!

*(***NORM*** sticks out his hand to* **GERALD**.*)*

GERALD. I don't shake hands.

NORM. I don't blame you. Number one way of spreading germs.

GERALD. Number two. Handrails are number one.

NORM. Good to know.

CORKY. *(To* **LAURA**.*)* I'm Norm's wife, Corky.

LAURA. I'm Gerald's wife, Laura.

GERALD. And I'm a guy with a vision of a wonderful night.

NORM. Ha! Us, too.

*(***GERALD*** is holding wine, offers it to* **CORKY**.*)*

GERALD. Small production winery in Santa Barbara. Eighty dollars.

CORKY. Wow, eighty.
(Then.) Something to drink?

LAURA. White wine is fine.

CORKY. Coming right up.

GERALD. Do you have a white that I could mix with Pellegrino? I love Pellegrino. The Coopers introduced us to Pellegrino. Remember that, Laura?

LAURA. You don't forget something like that.

CORKY. You know the Coopers?

NORM. We'd love to meet the Coopers.

CORKY. How long ago did you see them?

GERALD. Oh...four months ago?

*(***CORKY*** hands wine to both of them.)*

CORKY. Did you hear anything about him going off the rails?

    (**GERALD** *and* **LAURA** *glance at each other.*)

LAURA. *(Thinks.)* No...

GERALD. No...

    (Then.) The Coopers were interesting. On a certain level.

NORM. What do you mean?

GERALD. They were so well-behaved. Makes you suspicious.

LAURA. But they weren't hiding anything, did you think, Gerald?

GERALD. Maybe their true selves. Ha!

    (**GERALD** *starts to light a cigarette.*)

CORKY. Do you mind? Norm used to smoke. It's hard for him.

GERALD. Hard for all of us.

    (He puts it out, then, explosive.) SHIT!

    (Pause.)

CORKY. *(In the awkward silence.)* Oh look, it's night.

GERALD. Meteors are coming. Strangers from out of the blue. They remind me of me!

LAURA. *(Friendly, to* **NORM** *and* **CORKY**.*)* You should be aware that everything reminds him of him.

GERALD. It's kinda true.

    (**NORM** *walks over and picks up an eggplant. He starts bouncing it in his hand.*)

NORM. Love these eggplants by the way.

CORKY. Yes. They're lovely. Such an unusual gift.

NORM. So, thank you.

LAURA. Thank you...? For what?

CORKY. You didn't send them?

LAURA. What do you mean?

CORKY. We thought you sent them.

GERALD. Serious?

NORM. They came today. No card. Santa Barbara address. We figured from you.

GERALD. Sorry.

(Looks at them.)

I wonder why three.

NORM. I wonder why one.

(CORKY wanders over by LAURA.)

GERALD. Eggplants are a nightshade. Ever heard of deadly nightshade? Kill you like that. Tobacco's a nightshade. Point made. This is definitely a message.
(Re: the eggplants.) This is scary.

LAURA. Gerald can turn the brightest day into the darkest night.

GERALD. Norm, ever made eggplant lasagna?

LAURA. *(Privately, to CORKY.)* I bet Norm really loves your body.

(What? NORM is not sure what he heard.)

NORM. *(Soldiers on.)* I...find...eggplant hard to prepare. We don't buy much eggplant on our own. That's why we were excited to get these.

GERALD. First, you are an interesting conversationalist. I'll bet you get a lot of requests for that eggplant story. Second, eggplant lasagna is easy: ricotta, eggs, half cup Parmesan, oregano, mushrooms. But you gotta preheat the oven...four hundred degrees...

LAURA. Hey Chef Boyardee, you gonna list the whole recipe?

GERALD. Shut your stupid face.

LAURA. Eat me.

GERALD. You wish.

LAURA. I sure do, cowboy.

(Pause.)

CORKY. Well, what an interesting exchange of ideas.

(Lights out.)

Scene Five

(A jump back in time. Exterior of the house.
GERALD *and* **LAURA**. **GERALD** *is carrying a*
bottle of wine.)

GERALD. Perfect night for it, isn't it?

LAURA. Lovely. Did they get the eggplants?

GERALD. Delivered this afternoon.

LAURA. So. Who are they?

GERALD. Never met her, but he's handsome-ish so she
probably is too. That's the way it goes. Good-looking
guy, good-looking girl. Not so good-looking guy, not
so good-looking girl. Not so good-looking rich guy,
good-looking not so bright girl. Not so bright rich guy,
good-looking smart girl. Not so good-looking rich girl,
macho latent-homosexual guy.

(Then.) So how should we do this?

LAURA. Let's tell them I was obese.

GERALD. Ha! Nice. Good way to begin.

LAURA. I wish we'd had that one for the Coopers.

GERALD. The Coopers. The mighty Coopers. Who thought
they'd be so fragile?

LAURA. We can do better.

GERALD. Yes. Let's go for total collapse.

LAURA. *(Agreeing.)* Total collapse.

GERALD. So, you're obese.

LAURA. And you're his problem.

(Lights out.)

Scene Six

(Living room. Another jump back in time. The doorbell rings. **NORM** *and* **CORKY** *rise and rush to the door.)*

NORM. That must be they.

CORKY. They that must be. You know, I love to chat. And I haven't chatted for a while.

NORM. Hey? What's the last sixteen years been about?

CORKY. *(Hold hands, rushed.)* I understand that I have breached your feelings...

(The doorbell rings again.)

(Over his next line.) Here we go!

NORM. *(Rushed, as she walks away.)* I understand that you have recognized...

(The phone rings.)

Uh, the eight o'clock caller. Never fails. See who it is.

CORKY. *(Looking.)* It's blocked.

NORM. Oooh, fan-cy. Let the machine get it.

(A voice starts on the answering machine. **CORKY** *taps a button, turning it off.)*

(They open the door and greet their guests.)

Welcome.

CORKY. *(To* **LAURA.***)* Hello, I'm Norm's wife, Corky.

LAURA. I'm Gerald's wife, Laura.

GERALD. And I'm a guy with a vision of a wonderful night.

NORM. Ha! Us, too.

GERALD. *(Hands* **CORKY** *a bottle of wine.)* Small production winery in Santa Barbara. Eighty dollars.

CORKY. Wow, Eighty.

NORM. Well, you brought the good weather with you!

GERALD. *(Instructive.)* They've disproved that. Nobody brings weather with them. Simple science.

NORM. Well, it was just a figure of...

CORKY. What can I get you?

GERALD. White wine for both of us if you have it. With Pellegrino if you have it.

CORKY. We do.

NORM. There's some hors d'oeuvres on the table.

CORKY. And two dips. Regular and low-fat.

LAURA. When I have to choose between regular and low-fat, I understand the phrase "dark night of the soul."

NORM. Celery is actually minus calories.

GERALD. Not true. It's an old wives' tale.

LAURA. *(To* **GERALD.***)* Oh, really. Why is it a "wives'" tale? Because we're stupid?

GERALD. Relax.

LAURA. You relax, cowboy.

GERALD. Don't call me cowboy!
   (Then, to **CORKY.***)* See Laura here is sensitive about it because she was once obese.

LAURA. Jerry!

GERALD. Well, come on people know.

CORKY. Should I take the celery away?

LAURA. We can talk about it. I'm proud actually.

GERALD. Laura used to weigh three-hundred and ten.

CORKY. Huh.

LAURA. I weighed three-hundred and ten three times!

GERALD. She yo-yoed.

LAURA. I have underwear THIS big.

NORM. That seems impossible. You're so...tight.

   *(***CORKY*** eyes* **NORM.***)*

   (Breaking the silence.) Corky is a cannibal.

CORKY. NORM!

GERALD. *(Checks his watch, subtly looks at* **LAURA.***)* Oh yeah.

NORM. *(To* **CORKY.***)* We're just swapping intimacies.

LAURA. Is that true?

CORKY. *(Struggles.)* Well, yes, it is true. But I don't like the way you phrase it Norm, I am not a cannibal. I was once a cannibal.

NORM. Remember we looked this up, honey. It doesn't matter if you're actively doing it now. Even if you've only done it once, you remain a cannibal. Just semantics.

LAURA. If you don't mind I would love to hear the circumstances.

CORKY. I... I was... – I'm so sick of this story – I was lost in the Himalayas for forty-seven days with no food, my friend Kathy, and a dying Sherpa.

(A pause.)

LAURA. And?

NORM. And then there were none.

CORKY. Norm!

NORM. I would have done the same thing...

CORKY. I have to live with this...

NORM. Well come on baby it's old news, it happened seventeen years ago.

(To **GERALD** *and* **LAURA.***)* We're lucky it happened in the Himalayas. If it happened here it's six months in jail. There, it's just another day at the office.

CORKY. I just don't want people around here knowing.

NORM. It's been a problem.

LAURA. How?

NORM. She ate her friend Kathy.

LAURA. You must lie awake at night.

CORKY. No, that would be too easy. I developed exploding head syndrome. You can be just dozing off, and suddenly you think you've heard the loudest explosion of your life.

NORM. *(Contributing.)* And it's in her head. It can't be measured from the outside.

LAURA. Meaning?

CORKY. Meaning he's not convinced it's real.

NORM. How can you say that? Of course I believe you...

LAURA. How do you get rid of exploding head syndrome?

CORKY. Can't. It's not funded.

NORM. I can't even image what the poster for the fundraiser would look like.

> *(He makes an "exploding head" face and gesture.* **CORKY** *scowls at him.)*

CORKY. *(To* **LAURA**.*)* How did you come to be obese?

GERALD. She ate. She ate to punish me.

LAURA. I did.

CORKY. Why?

NORM. I know why. When women marry, they're expected to become mothers and take on huge responsibility. They're asked to give up their names and their lives as they've known it. Men just keep going to work, doing what they love. Laura was trying to punish him for that.

LAURA. That's very insightful, Norm. It hurt for a long time.

NORM. Because learning is pain.

CORKY. But pain is learning.

NORM. That was a beautiful insight Corky.

CORKY. I respect and value your comment.

NORM. Your growth is remarkable.

GERALD. What a load of shit.

LAURA. Shut your face, Gerald. Let them connect.

GERALD. Go fuck a dead goat.

LAURA. You'd like to watch.

GERALD. Is that the best you can do?

LAURA. *(Laser-like.)* You're bad at birthday gifts.
> *(Then, to* **NORM** *and* **CORKY**.*)* See? That's how you fight.

GERALD. She's so good at it!
> *(Then.)* Hey, let's get on outside.

NORM. It's meteor time!

LAURA. You two go. We'll fuss in here a bit.

NORM. Show her the upstairs closet.

CORKY. *(To* **LAURA**.*)* It's a walk-in.

GERALD. *(Heading for the outside, then stops.)* A walk-in? Now I'm torn. But let's get to the meteors. C'mon, new best friend.

> *(**GERALD** hustles **NORM** outside. We see them through the window.)*

LAURA. You and Norm seem so at ease with each other.

CORKY. Now, yeah. We really didn't know each other until year six. That's when I got depressed.

LAURA. When you get to know your husband you can't help but get depressed.

NORM. *(Offstage.)* …Oh, that was a beautiful one!

GERALD. *(Offstage. Yelling into the house.)* Holy shitstickies!

CORKY. But then we worked on it and we became soulmates.

LAURA. You worked on it?

CORKY. Reading, tapes. Seminars.

LAURA. Really.

CORKY. Learn the language. Men and women language.

LAURA. Oh right, I've heard of that. When Gerald and I had trouble we went to work on it too.

CORKY. What'd you do?

LAURA. Threesomes.

CORKY. You had a threesome?

LAURA. Gerald, me, and a stewardess.

CORKY. What did you think?

LAURA. I thought "lose the Gerald."

CORKY. Really!

LAURA. So then I did it with two other women.

CORKY. Wow. How did that go?

LAURA. We tried, but we just ended up talking.
(Then.) So, no more threesomes. Normal sex from now on.

NORM. *(Offstage.)* …Ho!!!!

GERALD. *(Offstage.)* Grab my balls and call me Robert!

LAURA. That's such a beautiful sound. Thank you for having us. I know it's hard to invite people into your home.

(**LAURA** *walks around, nosily. Finds a silverware box.*)

CORKY. That's what homes are for. To make people welcome and maybe take some of our joy and possibly share it with our guests.

LAURA. Yeah, right.

(*Laughs, then realizes she's serious.*)

Oh, yes.

(*Searches in silver box, then holds up a spoon.*)

This is such a lovely silver set.

CORKY. From my mother.

LAURA. Oh, so sweet. You ever been incarcerated?

CORKY. ...No...you?

LAURA. Minor. Kleptomania.

(*She gingerly puts back the spoon.*)

(*Lights out.*)

Scene Seven

(The backyard. **GERALD** *and* **NORM** *lie on chaise lounges, looking at the stars.)*

GERALD. *(A meteor streaks.)* Oh that was a beautiful one! *(Yelling into the house.)* Wow…!

NORM. *(Calling inside.)* Light show's on! You two better come out!

GERALD. You're missing it!

(Giggles from **LAURA** *and* **CORKY.***)*

NORM. They seem to get along…

GERALD. Oh yeah.

NORM. Hey, where're you from?

GERALD. Thank you so much for the invitation. I kinda feel like we invited ourselves.

NORM. Oh, no, no, it's fun. I don't know what's going on but I'm just going to go with it.
(Then.) How long have you two been married?

GERALD. Six months.

NORM. Really? You seem so used to each other.

GERALD. We just connected.

NORM. Mind if I be honest?

GERALD. Honesty is the only thing that gets me excited anymore.

NORM. You seem at each other's throats.

GERALD. May I be honest?

NORM. Sure…

GERALD. You seem not to be. What is that?

NORM. I'm glad you asked. We worked it out with help. You see we got tapes and understood that…

GERALD. If you don't mind I'd rather not. I have a built-in boredom detector.
(Then.) Corky seems great.

NORM. Thank you.

GERALD. Cute too.

NORM. Thanks.

GERALD. Very attractive.

NORM. Thank you.

GERALD. Must be nice.

NORM. It is.

GERALD. Nice hair.

NORM. Yeah...

GERALD. Good face.

NORM. Thanks.

GERALD. Tasty.

NORM. Huh...

GERALD. Nice figure.

NORM. She keeps it together.

GERALD. Pretty.

NORM. Oh yeah.

GERALD. And a nice body to go with.

NORM. Well...

GERALD. I mean it's not overworked.

NORM. She's a find.

GERALD. Nice bosoms.

NORM. *(Laughs unsurely.)* Yeah...

GERALD. Bazoombas.

NORM. Wait a min...

GERALD. My wife keeps herself together too.

NORM. She does.

GERALD. Yep, twelve wonderful years.

NORM. You said six months.

GERALD. Oh...we're back together six months. Couldn't stay apart. Turns out we're nuts about each other.
(Then.) Hey, let me show something. Laura! Come here and blow me!

LAURA. *(Enters.)* I thought that's why you learned yoga. Do it yourself.

(She exits.)

GERALD. See? I like the banter.

NORM. Let me show you something.
  (Calls.) Corky!

  (CORKY *enters.)*

Just felt like giving you a hug.

  (They hug.)

CORKY. Oh. Sweet.

  (She exits. **NORM** *looks at* **GERALD.***)*

NORM. See? That's our way.

GERALD. Big mistake.

NORM. Now how is a hug a big mistake?

GERALD. Not the hug. That's fine. So what who cares. But
  you broke it first. Never be the first one to break the
  hug. They have a memory...
  (Points to his brain, then, sinister.) ...A memory.
  (Then, calling.) You guys are missing it. It's incredible.
  You should get on out here.
  (Back to **NORM.***)* A memory.

  (The **WOMEN** *enter.)*

LAURA. We're not going to run out of meteors. It's the
  universe.

GERALD. It's why we're here. We should enjoy it.

NORM. I'm for it.
  (Affectionately, to **CORKY.***)* If we can stand the romance.

LAURA. I'm feeling frisky.

GERALD. The stars, the wine, warm breeze. Can't help it.
  More wine? Would anybody lick anything?

  (CORKY *bursts out laughing.)*

NORM. What, Corky?

CORKY. I... I thought... This is so embarrassing... I thought
  he said, "Would anybody lick anything."

LAURA. He did.

CORKY. So it was a slip of the tongue?

LAURA. Don't think so.

CORKY. *(Changing the subject.)* Well. I'll go get some ice.

NORM. We have plenty of ice.

CORKY. I would prefer to be out of ice right now.

> (**CORKY** *heads inside.*)

LAURA. I'll go with you.

> *(She exits to the living room.)*

NORM. *(To* **GERALD**.*)* Shall we?

> (**NORM** *gestures to go inside.* **GERALD** *stops* **NORM**.*)*

GERALD. Hey Norm, listen to this: if you want people to really open up, you have to get them alone. Let's each take some get-to-know-you time with the other spouse. Things come out. It's something I do that works. Let me send Laura out here, and I'll stay inside and rap with Corky.

NORM. Well, why not, I'd like to talk to Laura.

GERALD. She's hot isn't she?

NORM. *(Yes!)* Oh my God...!

GERALD. *(Cuts him off, acts mad, then.)* Hey! I'm just teasing you. You wait here.

NORM. I'll wait for Laura!

Scene Eight

> *(The living room.* **LAURA** *and* **CORKY** *enter from the kitchen.)*

LAURA. *(To* **CORKY.***)* Your kitchen is wonderful. I love that you've never fixed it up.

GERALD. Corky, can you make me a gin martini?

CORKY. Oh what a good idea. Fun. I think I can...let me see...

> **(GERALD** *throws* **LAURA** *a "get lost" look.)*

LAURA. *(Holding a drink.)* Is Norm outside? Poor lonely baby...

> **(LAURA** *exits to the lounges.)*

> **(CORKY** *turns toward a small bar and starts selecting ingredients. As she does,* **GERALD** *takes out a rubber hose, drug paraphernalia and shoots up.* **CORKY** *never notices.)*

CORKY. *(Mostly talking to herself.)* Gin martini. Shaken not stirred. Dry, bone-dry, or perfect. I'll decide. I don't really drink much anymore since I got healthy. That's odd to say, "I'm healthy." Of course I mean mentally healthy. I haven't had exploding head for months now.

GERALD. Uh-huh.

CORKY. I worked so hard to move from neurotic to normal. And Norm was so proud of me. But, Gerald, you know what I've been thinking lately?

GERALD. *(Nope.)* Uh-uh.

CORKY. Maybe neurotic *is* normal...and normal is really neurotic...

> **(GERALD** *multi-taps his arm to raise the vein.)*

No applause, no applause... You see when we act normal, we're really suppressing our favorite anxieties, and those anxieties really want to come out. So we're working twice as hard to be normal, when it's so easy, and stress-free, and relaxing, just to be completely insane. So normal is a big fake. In other words, maybe exploding head is a good thing because it's my natural state. I think I just made sense...

> (**GERALD** *snorts some cocaine.*)

This'll cure those sniffles.

> (**GERALD** *finishes his business and stows his drug paraphernalia in his coat. He leans back and grins at* **CORKY**.)

(Then.) ...And we add an olive...

> *(Hands him the martini.)*

Here it is.

(Then.) You okay?

GERALD. *(Takes a drink, then, off the taste.)* I was a little agitated but now I'm feeling quite languid.

CORKY. Well, good.

GERALD. You know, Corky...

CORKY. What. What's going on inside that brain of yours?

GERALD. Women...

CORKY. Yeah...

GERALD. ...Have a right to the extreme defense of their vaginas.

> *(They stare at each other.)*

CORKY. Uh-huh.

Thank you...

GERALD. See you've got this treasure trove down there. And men will lie to have it. So why should women play fair? If you've got what the most ruthless creatures on earth want you've got to be exceedingly clever to share it only with the right person. And who is the right person? Sometimes you find you're just standing there looking at him.

CORKY. *(She takes it all in, then, picking up his glass.)* Well, no more martinis for you.

> *(Lights fade on the living room.)*

Scene Nine

(Backyard. **NORM** *is sitting on one of the lounges. Music plays from an outdoor speaker.** **LAURA** *is dancing to it. The music eventually fades.)*

NORM. *(Sees her, then sees a meteor.)* Hey. Gerald is right. This is a real light show.

LAURA. Did Gerald suggest you spend time with me alone?

NORM. Uh...he did.

LAURA. He does that. He likes me to tempt men then report back.

NORM. I've read about that in trashy novels.

LAURA. Corky's making a drink for Gerald. I think they like each other.

NORM. Oh, that's great.

LAURA. You're so innocent.

NORM. I kinda like it that way.

LAURA. Don't you worry that he might come on to her?

NORM. No.

LAURA. Why not?

NORM. Because she and I are locked.

LAURA. You believe that?

NORM. I do.

LAURA. I was thinking the other day, recounting my life. I realized, no man has ever turned me down.

NORM. Wow. That's a score to keep.
(Then.) And I've never been turned down by a woman. Well, maybe a hundred times. And that was just Corky. Ha.

LAURA. Would you turn me down? Norm?

---

*A license to produce *Meteor Shower* does not include a performance license for any third-party or copyrighted music. Licensees should create an original composition or use music in the public domain. For further information, please see Music Use Note on page 3.

NORM. I would. I couldn't be unfaithful to Corky.

LAURA. That's rare.

NORM. No, it's not. That's most people.

LAURA. What's the harm?

NORM. The harm? Because then you and I would have a secret. Only Corky and I should have a secret.

LAURA. You're so honorable.

NORM. No, no. Just practical. Practicality generated by fear. I've got a lifetime with her. I can't compromise it for one evening.

(*A meteor streaks.*)

LAURA. One kiss won't hurt.

NORM. Yes it would.

LAURA. Not if you just happen to be standing where I'm kissing. You wouldn't even be a participant.

NORM. What?

(**LAURA** *looks around, peers into the house. She walks over to* **NORM,** *who stands motionless. She kisses him. They separate.*)

LAURA. How was it?

NORM. I don't know. I wasn't a participant.

LAURA. Norm?

NORM. Yeah?

LAURA. You just cheated on Corky.

NORM. No...

LAURA. Why would you do that?

NORM. I didn't!

LAURA. You've got a lifetime with her.

NORM. That's wasn't cheating.

LAURA. Some would say it is.

NORM. No...

LAURA. There's one sure way to find out.

NORM. What?

LAURA. Let's run it by Corky.

NORM. Oh, that's not a good idea.

LAURA. It's so sweet that you're guilty. Which just proves that you cheated on her.

NORM. No!

LAURA. And you're going to have to pay for that. So sorry.

(**NORM** *starts to go inside. The activity in the sky increases.*)

(*Looks at the sky.*) Gee, what's happening?

NORM. What?

LAURA. Look at the sky.

(**NORM** *pauses outside.*)

Wow, wow. Look at that. They're really coming fast.

NORM. They are. Like a lot.

LAURA. Look at that one.

NORM. Yeah.

LAURA. It almost looks like it's coming this way.

NORM. Wow, it is really getting hot out here.

(*He sits on the chaise. A meteor streaks.*)

It's like we're in a greenhouse.

(*While* **LAURA** *and* **NORM** *look at the heavens the lights come up on the living room, where* **GERALD** *and* **CORKY** *sit as in previous scene.*)

CORKY. Is it getting hot in here?

(*They start fanning themselves.*)

GERALD. It's like a furnace. Thank God I don't sweat.

CORKY. What is going on?

(*Suddenly, there is an explosion of lights and sound. In the darkness,* **NORM** *is in darkness.* **LAURA** *screams and runs inside.*)

LAURA. Oh God! ...Oh God! ...

CORKY. What is it?

LAURA. Well, Norm was just lying on the chaise lounge, and a meteor came down and went right through his stomach! He's got a hole in him the size of a dinner plate.

CORKY. Whaaat?

> *(Runs into the backyard.)*

(Offstage.) Oh no! Norm!

LAURA. *(To* GERALD*.)* Better than we could have hoped for.

GERALD. And we're just getting started!

> *(*CORKY *enters.)*

CORKY. *(Anguish.)* AHHHHH! Norm! Norm...

> *(She moans, walks around, then, through sobs:)*

OHHHH. Norm is gone! Oh Norm.

> *(A beat.)*

It's going to be so hard to be with other men but I guess I'll get used to it.

> *(She continues to sob and moan.)*

GERALD. I'll go take a look outside. See if there's anything left.

> *(*GERALD *exits.)*

CORKY. Oh my God.

LAURA. What?

CORKY. Gerald was right. Now there's one eggplant for each of us. The eggplants are omens.

LAURA. *(Pshaw.)* Omens. You'll be dating in six months.

CORKY. No! I made a solemn vow to never be with another man until death do us part!
(Then, realizing.) Oh!

LAURA. You want a drink?

CORKY. No. Vodka rocks.

LAURA. Do you want lime?

CORKY. Just rub it around the rim.

LAURA. How many times have I heard that.

(CORKY laughs, realizes it's inappropriate, then turns it into a cry. GERALD re-enters.)

GERALD. *(Pained.)* Ahhhh. Norm is gone! ...We've lost our Norm!

LAURA. You two were inseparable.

GERALD. He was my best friend!

LAURA. *(Hands CORKY the drink.)* This'll help.

GERALD. What do I do now? How do *I* live?

LAURA. *(To GERALD.)* God you loved him.

CORKY. I can redecorate.

GERALD. We were like brothers.

LAURA. You were. Get ready for a flood of memories.

GERALD. Oh, Norm!

LAURA. He'll always be with us!

CORKY. Well, what do we do now? It's not even that late.

(Lights out.)

Scene Ten

(The backyard. There are the two chaise lounges, but now one with a two-foot hole in the cushion clear through to the ground where a meteor has fallen through. Smoke and embers emanate from the hole.)

*(**CORKY** stares at it, whimpering. **GERALD** enters.)*

GERALD. Laura's lying down. I put her on your bed. I hope that's okay.

CORKY. How could this happen?

GERALD. Why couldn't it have been me? Please God, make it be me.

(He looks heavenward. Not today, he guesses. **CORKY** *sobs quietly into her handkerchief.)*

A piece of rock, traveling for eons...aimed millions of years ago at this spot...not headed for Norm, he just happened to be in the place where it landed.

CORKY. I didn't get a chance to say what I wanted to say to him.

GERALD. Me either.

CORKY. What would you have said?

GERALD. Huh?

CORKY. What would you have said?

GERALD. Oh. I would have told him...I would have liked to bathe in his normalcy. He was so normal.

CORKY. Normal Norm.

GERALD. He was a flatline.

CORKY. *(Bingo.)* Yes!

GERALD. Norman. Norm-Man. I would've loved to have been in his head for a day, to understand what it's like to have no inner life. What would you have said?

CORKY. Him. Things about him. His laugh. And he was just learning how to cry. I loved that.

GERALD. Crying is so manly. Currently. You must have loved it when he held you and cried those big manly tears.

CORKY. Oh yes, I did.

(Then.) He had just bought these chairs. If he could see them now he'd be so upset. We made love on these chairs.

GERALD. That's what you do with a new chair.

CORKY. Norm had just unpacked them and I came out to look, and suddenly we both had the urge. It was funny.

GERALD. Funny ha ha or funny peculiar?

CORKY. Funny peculiar. I don't know funny ha ha.

GERALD. I don't believe that.

CORKY. Where did you put him?

GERALD. Why? You're not going to eat him, are you?

CORKY. NO! How could I think of food at a time like this?

GERALD. He's in the garage.

CORKY. *(Teary.)* Oh! Oh. That's so perfect. He had just organized the garage. He was so proud.

GERALD. It did seem extremely organized. And your car was gleaming. Practically incandescent. Like it had just been intensely polished.

CORKY. Oh no, that's impossible.

GERALD. Why?

CORKY. It's just impossible. When I first met Norm, he had a ritual. Every third Sunday, he would park his car on the street and wax it. Carnauba, that was the best wax.

GERALD. Good reliable brand. And, it's edible.

CORKY. Well, anything's edible.

(Going on.)

But then something happened. Over the years cars evolved. They started coming with a hard-shell transparent gloss. They were indelible. For a while, Norm pretended. But one Sunday, I looked out and he was there waxing but not with his usual fervor. And I said, "Norm, are you all right?" And he looked at me and said, "I feel redundant." And he picked up his chamois, put it in his...bucket thing...oh what do you call that?

GERALD. Car shampoo caddy.

CORKY. Yes. Car shampoo caddy. Then he walked into the garage, and never waxed again.

GERALD. I hope he experienced life.

CORKY. A meteor. Struck by a meteor. The odds must be astronomical. Oh, that's funny.

(Laughs a bit.)

Astronomical...and a meteor. I didn't even intend it.

GERALD. You do know funny ha ha.

CORKY. You know, I guess I do.

(Looks at the death lounge.)

Thank you, Norm. In your death you brought me laughter.

GERALD. Once he took you. He took you for the first time, remember?

CORKY. I do.

GERALD. That loss of reason – you gave up reason and surrendered.

CORKY. Yes.

GERALD. You were loved; you were overcome...and you capitulated.

(He snuggles her. She responds.)

CORKY. No, no. Norm's death lounge is still smoldering.

GERALD. Norm would want it this way.

CORKY. (She starts handling him.) Yes...he would...wait, how could he possibly want it this way? My you have big muscles.

GERALD. He loved it when you were this close to him.

CORKY. He did.

GERALD. He held you like this...

CORKY. Yes, exactly like this.

GERALD. And you wanted him.

CORKY. I did.

   (Then.) Have you ever been wanted? Really wanted?

GERALD. Not until now.

CORKY. By whom?

GERALD. By youm.

CORKY. I know.

GERALD. You want me. This doesn't make sense.

CORKY. It doesn't make sense.

> *(They creep back on the lounge, perfectly situated over Norm's "death hole," which* **CORKY** *momentarily falls into: "Whoa.")*

GERALD. But sense is not a thing meant to be made.

CORKY. No, it's not!

> *(She pulls him toward her and they start seducing one another.)*

GERALD. Corky, meet Gerald.

> *(He lies on top of her.)*
>
> *(Lights dim.)*

Scene Eleven

(Backyard. **LAURA** *dancing seductively.)*

(Dance music continues.* The music rouses **CORKY***, who has been ravaged.)*

CORKY. *(Sees her.)* Laura.

LAURA. Are you doing any better, honey?

CORKY. No.

LAURA. Tell me.

CORKY. What I've done.

LAURA. You haven't done anything.

CORKY. Yes, I have. Gerald came out here and you were upstairs and it was like he brought out this part of me that...that...

LAURA. That what?

CORKY. ...That I didn't even know was there. And all these things were coming up inside me and all of a sudden...

> *(Suddenly* **CORKY***'s body jolts. Then it jolts again. She points to her head.)*

LAURA. What is it?!

CORKY. MY HEAD IS EXPLODING. OH GOD THERE IT IS AGAIN. MY HEAD IS EXPLODING.

LAURA. You just need to relax.

CORKY. No, I can't! I've hurt you! And Norm. And myself.

LAURA. Shh.

> *(Boom. Another explosion in her head.)*

CORKY. You seriously can't hear that?

> *(She moans, sits, calms.)*

Marriage has always been so difficult for me.

LAURA. Easier for you now.

---

*A license to produce *Meteor Shower* does not include a performance license for any third-party or copyrighted music. Licensees should create an original composition or use music in the public domain. For further information, please see Music Use Note on page 3.

CORKY. Norm and I worked so hard. How do you do it?

LAURA. You learn. Little things, they add up. Like, never be the first one to break a hug.

CORKY. I can see that.

(*Dawning awareness.*) I think I did that to Norm. I broke first!

LAURA. Corky, you're so sensitive.

(*Then.*) Where did you grow up?

CORKY. Do we ever grow up?

LAURA. Corky, you have a way of making a cliché new again.

(*Then.*) Where did you grow up?

CORKY. Cleveland. Where are you from?

LAURA. Tierra del Fuego.

CORKY. Tierra del Fuego? You just don't seem like you're from Tierra del Fuego.

LAURA. I hear that a lot.

CORKY. What language do they speak?

LAURA. Tierra del Fueganese.

CORKY. Can you speak it?

LAURA. Si.

(*Then.*) Si, si.

CORKY. Can you say...complex things?

LAURA. Oh, Si. Si, complexico.

CORKY. That's wonderful.

LAURA. It can be a burden. There were two del Fuegan men who worked in the *Vogue* office. They didn't know I spoke del Fueganese. They said awful things about me. Mostly soccer metaphors, "I'd like to score in her goal." Things like that.

CORKY. That's awful.

LAURA. Then one day I said to them, "¿Por qué no ponen sus pollas en un sacapuntas eléctrico?"

CORKY. What does that mean?

LAURA. "Why don't you two put your dicks in the electric pencil sharpener."

    (They both chuckle.)

And you know who they fired? Me.

    (Fingers **CORKY***'s dress, lingering on her breasts.)*

This is nice this fabric.

CORKY. Well, thank you. There's this really cute store in town...

LAURA. *(Sees a meteor.)* Oh, did you see that?

    (**LAURA** *moves closer to* **CORKY.***)*

CORKY. I did. Gerald is so right; they're heart-stopping.
    (Then.) Oh, Laura. I just realized the explosions are gone.

LAURA. Yes.

    (She puts her arm around her.)

CORKY. That feels good.

LAURA. Just a caress.

CORKY. I feel better.

LAURA. I know.

    (**LAURA** *nuzzles her cheek.)*

CORKY. You're warm.

LAURA. You need warmth.

CORKY. I do.

LAURA. You need it now.

CORKY. *(Sees a meteor.)* Oh, you missed it.

    (They stand apart.)

LAURA. I want you.

CORKY. I know.

LAURA. Come.

CORKY. I've never done this before.

LAURA. I'll be your guide.

    *(**CORKY** lies down on the chaise.)*

Watch the hole.

    *(**LAURA** joins her. Cuddle. Cross legs.)*

    (Lights out.)

Scene Twelve

(Living room, later.)

*(**LAURA**. She's busy at the drinks cart with a cocktail shaker.)*

*(**NORM** enters from the garage. He has a large hole in his stomach, clear through to his back, with guts hanging out. There is smoke coming out of the hole.)*

(He's groggy. Wondering where he is. Staggers. Slowly he figures it out.)

*(**LAURA** turns, sees him, surprised.)*

NORM. Hey Laura. How you doin'?

(He sits, but it hurts. He pops back up.)

LAURA. I'm fine, but I thought you were dead.

*(**LAURA** walks toward him with a drink in her hand.)*

NORM. Sometimes you have to hit bottom before you can turn around.

(He takes the drink in her hand.)

Thank you.

(Then.) Laura, do you mind if I spill my guts a bit? I was out there in the garage, pretty dead...

(He takes several swigs.)

...and I'm floating up toward the light in the sky...the whole thing...

(He coughs. Water squirts out of his stomach.)

...and I got to thinking about you and Gerald and this question kept pulling at me...

(He coughs again, more water squirts.)

...pulling me back to life.

LAURA. What?

NORM. What's with the aggression?

LAURA. Oh. We like the game.

NORM. What's the game?

LAURA. Strike first.

NORM. Why so cynical? Why not a little optimism?

LAURA. Optimism gives you disappointment. Cynicism gives you the world.
(*Then, calls.*) Gerald! Get some ointment!

(**GERALD** *enters.*)

GERALD. Why? Did you hurt…

(*Sees* **NORM.**)

Holy shit! Gee, you're resilient!

(**CORKY** *enters, still romantically charged from her experience with* **LAURA.**)

CORKY. (*Enters seductively.*) Laura, I just remembered…
(*Sees* **NORM.**) AHHHHH! Yikes! Norm, what are you doing here? You're supposed to be dead.

NORM. I'm tired of being what I'm "supposed" to be.

CORKY. Well, you gotta make up your mind! I was making plans.

LAURA. This is unfair to Corky.

NORM. I don't care what's unfair to Corky!

CORKY. You never have!

NORM. Yes, I have!

LAURA. I doubt it.

NORM. (*To* **LAURA.**) Butt out!

LAURA. (*Annoyed.*) Give her a break. You were dead on arrival when she slept with me and Gerald.

NORM. You slept with both of them?

CORKY. I was mourning you!
(*Then.*) Uh-oh. Uh-oh.

NORM. Here we go.

CORKY. My head is exploding!

NORM. (*Cynical.*) Oh, exploding head. So phony!

CORKY. *(Points to her head.)* Aha! So you *don't* think it's real!

NORM. It's in your head.

    (Points to his stomach.) This is real! You've gone insane.

CORKY. Eat me.

NORM. Like you did to Kathy?

GERALD. Good one.

CORKY. You never liked my mother.

NORM. Where did that come from?

GERALD. *(To* **NORM,** *pointing to his own head.)* They have a "memory"!

NORM. Screw you!

CORKY. *(To* **NORM** *and* **GERALD.***)* Por qué no ponen sus pollas en un sacapuntas eléctrico!

    (High-five between **LAURA** *and* **CORKY.***)*

NORM. We don't even have an electric pencil sharpener!

LAURA. Better than we could have hoped for.

    *(***NORM** *takes a swig. More water.* **CORKY***'s head explodes. Chaos.)*

GERALD. Total collapse! The bug flux has been achieved!

Scene Thirteen

(A jump back in time to the first scene. **CORKY** *enters.)*

CORKY. Norm, they're here in fifteen minutes.

(She exits to the kitchen.)

(Exterior of the house. **GERALD** *and* **LAURA**.*)*

GERALD. Perfect night for it, isn't it?

LAURA. Lovely. Did they get the eggplants?

GERALD. Delivered this afternoon.

LAURA. I love the eggplants.

GERALD. Before you knock someone over you have to put them off balance.

*(***NORM** *enters from upstairs. The hole in* **NORM** *is gone.)*

NORM. It's on the tip of my tongue...something like Death to the Cuckoo.

CORKY. *(Entering with hors d'oeuvres.)* To Kill a Mockingbird.

NORM. Thank you!

(The phone rings.)

Oh, eight o'clock caller. Always at dinner...

LAURA. Gerald, where's the wine?

GERALD. Oh... I left it in the back seat. A rare mistake.

LAURA. A rare admission.

(They walk back to the car.)

*(***CORKY** *looks at Caller ID unit.)*

CORKY. It's blocked.

NORM. Pick it up. It might be them.

*(***CORKY** *picks up the phone. We can hear the squeak of the voice on the other end of the phone.)*

CORKY. Hello? Uh-huh... This is she. Well, we've wanted to meet you for a long time, too.

(Loud whisper.) It's the Coopers!

NORM. *(Contained celebration.)* The Coopers?

CORKY. *(Into phone.)* Yes, we did invite them. They should be here in a few minutes... Uh-huh. Uh-huh.

(Listens, then covers the phone.)

It's Nancy Cooper. She heard we were having the Newmans over and she's calling to warn us.

NORM. *(Under his breath.)* Warn us?

CORKY. *(Into phone.)* Should we uninvite them? ...What do you mean they're not visitors?

NORM. Not visitors?

CORKY. Well, what should we do? Okay. Really. Really. We will. We definitely will. Thank you.

NORM. We will what?

CORKY. She said defend.

NORM. Defend?

CORKY. Defend and protect.

NORM. Why?

CORKY. Norm, do you know how Velcro works?

NORM. Uh, Velcro. Tiny little hooks and eyes, right?

CORKY. Right. And we, us, are like Velcro.

NORM. Go ahead.

CORKY. When we first met and were so crazy for each other – little hooks went in. And when we dated, and moved in, and bought a house, little hooks...going in, binding us together.

NORM. And when you like my jokes...

CORKY. What jokes?

*(**NORM** laughs.)*

See, more hooks just went in. But when we had trouble and difficulty you know what happened?

NORM. The hooks came undone...

CORKY. No. No. More hooks went in. Trouble or happiness, hooks. Even the bad times bonded us. And we became a couple.

NORM. We did. We are.

CORKY. And you know what's happening now?

NORM. What?

CORKY. Someone is coming over who wants to rip that Velcro apart.

> *(There is a pause while* **NORM** *computes this.)*

Defend and protect.

NORM. Defend and protect.

> *(We see* **GERALD** *and* **LAURA** *return and head up the walkway,* **GERALD** *with the wine.)*
>
> *(Ding dong.)*

CORKY & NORM. Defend and protect.

> *(***GERALD** *and* **LAURA** *enter.)*

NORM. Welcome!

> *(***NORM** *coughs into his hand and quickly shakes* **GERALD**'s *hand.* **GERALD** *stares at it.)*

CORKY. *(To* **LAURA**.*)* Hello, I'm Norm's wife, Corky. You?

LAURA. I'm Gerald's wife, Laura.

CORKY. Nice to meet you, Gerald's wife.

GERALD. *(Hands* **CORKY** *a bottle of wine.)* Small production winery in Santa Barbara. Eighty dollars.

CORKY. Oh, I know this wine. It's four dollars. Would you like a drink? Not this.

> *(She stows the wine in a low cabinet.)*

LAURA. I'd love to have a drink. I'm more fun to be around.

GERALD. You're telling me. Sometimes getting her legs open takes an act of God.

CORKY. *(To* **GERALD**.*)* And I guess you're just not God. What can I get you?

GERALD. White wine for both of us if you have it. With Pellegrino or club soda... I prefer Pellegrino...

> (**CORKY** *cuts him off by handing him a straight white wine.*)

CORKY. No one cares. There's some celery on the table.

NORM. Celery is actually minus calories.

GERALD. I heard they disproved that.

NORM. *(Mocking.)* "I heard they disproved that."

> (**GERALD** *looks at* **NORM** *oddly.*)

LAURA. Still, I'm going to resist.

GERALD. See, Laura here was once obese.

LAURA. Jerry!

GERALD. Well, come on people know. Laura used to weigh three-hundred and ten.

NORM. You still have a little of it on you.

LAURA. I do?

CORKY. Just a bit.

> (**CORKY** *makes a "wide hips" gesture.*)

LAURA. Oh.

GERALD. *(Taking a bite of the hors d'oeuvres.)* Hmm. Tasty. What is this?

CORKY. Petrale crab from Chile. Well, technically it's rodent.

> (**GERALD** *spits it out.*)

LAURA. Well, here we are, just the four of us.

> (*Awkward silence.*)

CORKY. Norm has an enormous dick.

> (**NORM** *smiles proudly over at them.*)

GERALD. How enormous?

CORKY. It's been photographed by Mapplethorpe.

LAURA. How did he hear about it?

NORM. Word of mouth. I inherited it from my grandfather. It seems to skip a generation.

CORKY. It's like having a third person in the house.

GERALD. That must be unpleasant, Corky.

CORKY. *(Ironic.)* Oh, yeah. Yeah. Really unpleasant! Ha!

> (**CORKY** *high-fives* **NORM**.)
>
> *(Pause.)*

NORM. Well, here we are, just the five of us!

> (**NORM** *laughs at his joke.*)

LAURA. Corky, I'd love to look around the house.

CORKY. Twat?

LAURA. That's funny, I thought you said...

CORKY. Twat. Let me show you around the kitchen.

> (**CORKY** *pushes* **LAURA** *out.*)
>
> (**GERALD** *and* **NORM** *walk to the outside.*)

NORM. They seem to get along. How long have you two been together?

GERALD. Years.

NORM. Really? It seems new.

GERALD. It does?

NORM. Yeah. She doesn't seem exactly with you.

GERALD. How do you mean?

> *(They walk to the outdoors.)*

NORM. Oh, the way she dresses, kind of out there, offering it around.

GERALD. Laura?

NORM. She rolls her eyes when you say things. It's funny. We laugh, but it's a little disrespectful.

GERALD. Laura doesn't roll her eyes behind my back.

> *(They are now in the backyard.)*

NORM. No, no. Not always. Sometimes it's just implied. Look if I'm saying something I shouldn't... Sit down.

> *(He offers* **GERALD** *the chaise lounge.* **GERALD** *sits.* **NORM** *puts one leg up on it, his crotch*

uncomfortably close to **GERALD**. **GERALD** *looks slightly nervous.*)

NORM. Such a beautiful evening. You know, in space, meteors are just rocks, some the size of pebbles, but on Earth, a pebble can create a dazzling light show, then burn out. Like you.

GERALD. What do you...?

NORM. You are a very poetic person. You came here tonight to see the meteors. Not many men would do that. Not real men.

GERALD. I guess I'm sensitive.

(**NORM** *massages* **GERALD**'s *shoulders.*)

NORM. Very rare. Rare for a male to be sensitive.

(*He starts massaging* **GERALD**'s *thighs.*)

Wow. Now why would you work out one thigh and not the other?

GERALD. I uh...

NORM. You're not comfortable with this, are you? Gerald, you have to learn to say, "I'm not comfortable with this." When Corky and I learned to say that our marriage improved. Take a baby step. Say it for me.

GERALD. I can't say that. It's so wimpy.

NORM. No, No. Great phrase. At one point I even told Corky that I was uncomfortable with things that I was actually comfortable with. Then I could show her how I could change, by becoming comfortable with things I was already comfortable with. It worked so well, our romance blossomed. I knew I had made her happy. Now I always lie for her happiness. Is that what you do? Do you lie to Laura for her happiness?

GERALD. I tell her the flat-out truth...

NORM. So I guess Laura will be leaving you soon.

GERALD. You mean it's a bad idea?

NORM. Let me give you some advice. If you know you're going to eventually say yes to something, say yes right away. Don't start by saying no and then say yes.

GERALD. What exactly?

NORM. Let's say she wants to take a driving trip through wine country... Now maybe that's the last thing on earth you want to do, driving from chateau to chateau...

GERALD. *(Liking it.)* I could see...

> *(During the following speech,* **NORM** *lies next to* **GERALD** *seductively, becoming more and more forward.)*

NORM. ...Tasting wines you don't know anything about and getting looped before noon no matter how little you sip and then steering a car in the blinding sun on winding roads. By five p.m. you're so wiped out – and you've got these bottles rattling around in the back seat – all you want to do is just lie in bed and watch the game, but the B and B you're staying at is so crunchy with granola they don't have a TV, and it's so silent in your room all you can hear is the sound of your own blood...

> *(Intertwining with* **GERALD**, *rubbing his chest.)*

...whooshing, whooshing, whooshing. Then later, you go to a restaurant where the service is so slow you could read Proust between courses, and by the end of the night you've had so much alcohol you're really in a walking-around coma. But somewhere in the back of your mind, no matter how much you don't want to go, you know you're going to end up on a driving trip in wine country. So she doesn't need to hear a litany of all the reasons you don't want to go since you're going anyway.

GERALD. That sounds like good advice.

NORM. Happy wife, happy who gives a shit.

> *(Then.)* Hey Gerald, one thing. I've been straight my whole life, but now, I completely get it.

> *(Blackout.)*

Scene Fourteen

(The living room. **CORKY** *and* **LAURA** *are discovered on the sofa.)*

GERALD. *(Yelling, offstage.)* Hey, you two! You better come out...!

NORM. *(Yelling, offstage.)* It's 10:15!

LAURA. They're like two children.

CORKY. It always amazes me how men can turn so quickly into boys.

LAURA. Aren't you glad you're not a man?

CORKY. Oh, so relieved. I couldn't stand all the advantages.

*(**CORKY** lies back on the sofa, takes off her shoes, and rests them on **LAURA**.)*

LAURA. You and Norm seem bonded.

CORKY. Well, there were troubled years. But then we had our kids.

LAURA. Aw, what are their names?

CORKY. Oh jeez...let's see. I wanna say Lisa...or Lynette, one of those, then something...uh...Beaver?
(Calling.) Norm, do we have a kid named Beaver?

NORM. *(Calling, offstage.)* We do!

CORKY. I thought so. They're grown and out of the house now.

LAURA. Oh, how old are they?

CORKY. Nine and seven. You haven't had anything to eat all night.

*(**CORKY** picks up a piece of celery with her toes, offers it to **LAURA**. **LAURA** takes it nervously.)*

Gerald seems nice.

LAURA. He isn't. I'm nice.

CORKY. Yeah? Why are you really here? To rip us apart?

LAURA. Oh, don't worry about me. I'm just here all shapely in your room.

(**NORM** *enters.*)

NORM. *(To* **CORKY.***)* Your turn.

CORKY. Oh, I'd love to visit with Gerald.

LAURA. I'll come too.

CORKY. *(To* **LAURA.***)* Stay!

NORM & CORKY. *(Not in unison, swapping lines.)* So long, lovebird! Little honey pie, sweetie baby...moogie moogie moogie, you're my little baby and I going to wash you in the sink...

(**CORKY** *exits.*)

NORM. Does Corky irritate you as much as she does me?

LAURA. I'm starting to like her.

NORM. Laura. Luscious Laura. Yummy, yummy Laura. Hey. Idea. What if exactly one month from today you and I met in Rome atop the Spanish Steps. Wait, never mind, I've got that dinner.

LAURA. Norm...what if you were to kiss me? Right now.

NORM. You mean like this?

(*Rushes to her, big wet kiss...then...*)

Oh my God, what have I done? I was unfaithful! I've never been unfaithful!

LAURA. Yes, you were unfaithful to Corky.

NORM. No! No! I was not unfaithful to Corky! I was unfaithful to Gerald!

Scene Fifteen

*(Outside, by the chaise lounges, which are whole. **GERALD** and **CORKY. CORKY** dances, à la Laura.)*

GERALD. *(Watching her.)* Sweet.

CORKY. Thank you.

GERALD. It's a lawless night.

CORKY. *(Playing dumb.)* I think I know what you mean.

> *(**CORKY** eyes the lounge, checks her watch, looks skyward.)*

GERALD. There are nights when something, an act, is so wrong, but another night, the same action is without judgement.

CORKY. I know. Some nights, one's standards just relax.

GERALD. They do relax.

CORKY. But I can't. Norm. Everything.

GERALD. Corky, listen. Advice.

CORKY. What, Jerry?

GERALD. Don't be a fucking virgin.

> *(Pause.)*

CORKY. Oh my God. That's so funny.

GERALD. What?

CORKY. A fucking virgin. It's an oxymoron.

GERALD. Don't call me a...

CORKY. You are so clever. The way you're able to contour language without confronting hyperbole.

GERALD. People tell me that.

> *(**GERALD** walks away from her.)*

CORKY. Where are you going?

GERALD. Women talk about what it's like to enter my sphere. I want you to have that experience.

> *(He beckons her toward him. She walks to him slowly.)*

CORKY. *(Experiencing walking into his sphere.)* Oooh.

> *(Walks more, feels it again.)*

Oooh! What kind of spell have you cast on me?

GERALD. I just have it. Is it getting warm out here?

CORKY. *(Caressing.)* My temperature's rising.

> *(Looks inside to see if anyone's coming.)*

We'll have to be quick.

GERALD. My speciality.

> **(GERALD** *lies down on the "wrong" chaise lounge.)*
>
> *(The sky gets agitated.* **CORKY** *checks it out.)*

CORKY. *(She pats the appropriate lounge.)* Oh. Not that one. Lie on the sexy one.

GERALD. *(He moves.)* I can feel your heat from here.

> *(She starts backing up.)*

CORKY. I can feel *your* heat!

> *(The lights start to fade.* **CORKY** *checks her watch periodically.)*

(Then, she waves him over.) Oh, a little to your left.

GERALD. *(He adjusts.)* Kooky.

> *(Ominous sounds and lights from the sky.)*

CORKY. *(Then.)* Gerald meet Corky.

> *(The stage lights go dark. Then there is the sound and fury of a meteor hitting.)*

Scene Sixteen

> *(The living room with* **LAURA** *and* **NORM** *and*
> **CORKY**. **GERALD** *appears, staggering, at the*
> *backyard door, smoke emanating from his*
> *jacket. The jacket is in tatters.)*

GERALD. What a fun night!

LAURA. Yes, we've had a wonderful evening. But I feel like I
feel like we've overstayed our welcome.

NORM. Oh no. That's impossible. You were never welcome.

CORKY. Well, good night, Gerald. Good night, Laura.

> **(CORKY** *walks directly to* **LAURA**. *She delivers*
> *a lingering good night kiss.* **GERALD** *looks on*
> *nervously as it goes on too long.)*

NORM. Niiiicccceee.

GERALD. I'm not comfortable with this.
(Then, elated.) Hey, I said it!

NORM. You just took an important baby step!

GERALD. Feels good.
(Enjoying saying it.) I'm not comfortable with this.

> **(LAURA** *lowers her arms and silverware falls*
> *out. She looks down at it, picks it up.)*

CORKY. Laura, could I get you a drink for the road?

LAURA. Sure.

GERALD. Come on, Laura, give it a rest. Wait till we get
home.

> **(GERALD** *realizes what he's said. They walk*
> *downstage and enter "talking mode," à la*
> *Norm and Corky.)*

LAURA. I honor your perspective and you should go fuck
yourself.

GERALD. Got it.

NORM. Hey, you never told us where you're from!

CORKY. Oh, Norm. Don't you know? They're ourselves. They came to teach us a lesson.

LAURA. If you don't deal with your subconscious it will deal with you.

NORM. Oh yeah.

Oh, and we want you to have these.

(He picks up the eggplants and hands them to **GERALD** *and* **LAURA**.*)*

GERALD. A lovely memory of an important evening.

LAURA. Si, si. Eggplantico.

(They take the eggplants.)

GERALD. Well, we hope we can see you again sometime.

*(***NORM** *and* **CORKY** *usher them out.)*

CORKY & NORM. Oh, no, no. We're booked...very busy...got that dinner...

CORKY, NORM, LAURA & GERALD. Good night...good night.

*(***GERALD** *and* **LAURA** *are out the door.* **NORM** *and* **CORKY** *celebrate.)*

NORM. We did it.

CORKY. We did.

(Then.) Norm, I have to ask you something.

NORM. Sure baby.

CORKY. Did you wax the car today?

NORM. I did.

CORKY. Tell me.

NORM. When I woke up this morning, I had a premonition that today the different parts of me would be united. And I would become a whole person. And when you went into town I went out to the garage, got out that... that...uh...

CORKY. Car shampoo caddy.

NORM. Right. And went to work. I polished till I could see myself. Really see myself. And it felt good.

CORKY. That's nice. I'm glad.

NORM. More meteors?

CORKY. Let's.

> *(They amble outside. The chaise lounge still has its hole. They take in the sky. She turns to him.)*

(Looking at the sky.) Oh my.

NORM. Wonderful.

CORKY. Norm, Remember when Laura first came in and she made this...um, remark about our house?

NORM. Yeah...

CORKY. Well, you glanced over and gave me a look. A tiny, quick look.

NORM. Yes. You gave me the look back.

CORKY. And I thought, "This is what marriage is all about."

NORM. They couldn't rip us apart.

CORKY. Nothing energizes a marriage more than a common enemy.

NORM. Who said that?

CORKY. I did.

NORM. It sounds like you.

CORKY. I love you, Norm.

> *(There's a pause. Then:)*

You don't have to say it back. It will just sound like you're saying it because I said it...

NORM. I love you.

CORKY. Thank you.
You know what I'd like to do? Just the two of us. Take a trip through wine country.

NORM. *(Tiny pause.)* Nothing better.

(He goes to her, they hug, motionless. They stand for a while, neither wanting to "break the hug." Awkwardly long. They never break. Ending music begins.*)

(The lights dim.)

---

*A license to produce *Meteor Shower* does not include a performance license for any third-party or copyrighted music. Licensees should create an original composition or use music in the public domain. For further information, please see Music Use Note on page 3.